THE CAT THAT DISAPPEARED

MY FIRST GRAPHIC NOVELS ARE PUBLISHED BY STONE ARCH BOOKS
A CAPSTONE IMPRINT
151 GOOD COUNSEL DRIVE, P.O. BOX 669
MANKATO, MINNESOTA 56002
WWW.CAPSTONEPUB.COM

Library of Congress Cataloging-in-Publication data is available on the
Library of Congress website.

Library Binding: 978-1-4342-1887-2
Paperback: 978-1-4342-2282-4

Summary: Ava's cat goes missing right before the pet show. Ava, Clair, and Caleb
have to find Oatmeal before the show begins.

Art Director: Bob Lentz
Graphic Designer: Emily Harris
Production Specialist: Michelle Biedscheid

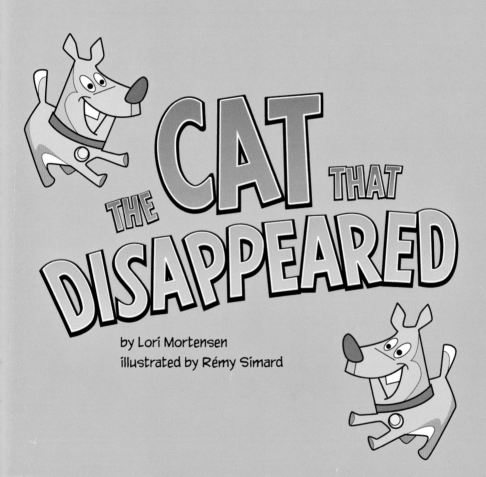

THE CAT THAT DISAPPEARED

by Lori Mortensen

illustrated by Rémy Simard

STONE ARCH BOOKS
a capstone imprint

HOW TO READ A GRAPHIC NOVEL

Graphic novels are easy to read. Boxes called panels show you how to follow the story. Look at the panels from left to right and top to bottom.

Read the word boxes and word balloons from left to right as well. Don't forget the sound and action words in the pictures.

The pictures and the words work together to tell the whole story.

Ava was bored. So was her cat, Oatmeal.

Then Ava had an idea.

She grabbed her phone and called her friends.

Clair brought her dog. Caleb brought his snake.

They made a stage in Ava's backyard. They also made signs.

They set up chairs.

But by showtime, Oatmeal had disappeared.

Ava and her friends searched outside.
Ava looked in the big tree.

Clair looked in the garden.

Caleb looked under the car.

No one could find Oatmeal.

Ava and her friends searched inside. Ava looked under the sofa.

Clair looked under the bed.

Caleb looked in the closet.

They still couldn't find Oatmeal.

Ava had a new idea.

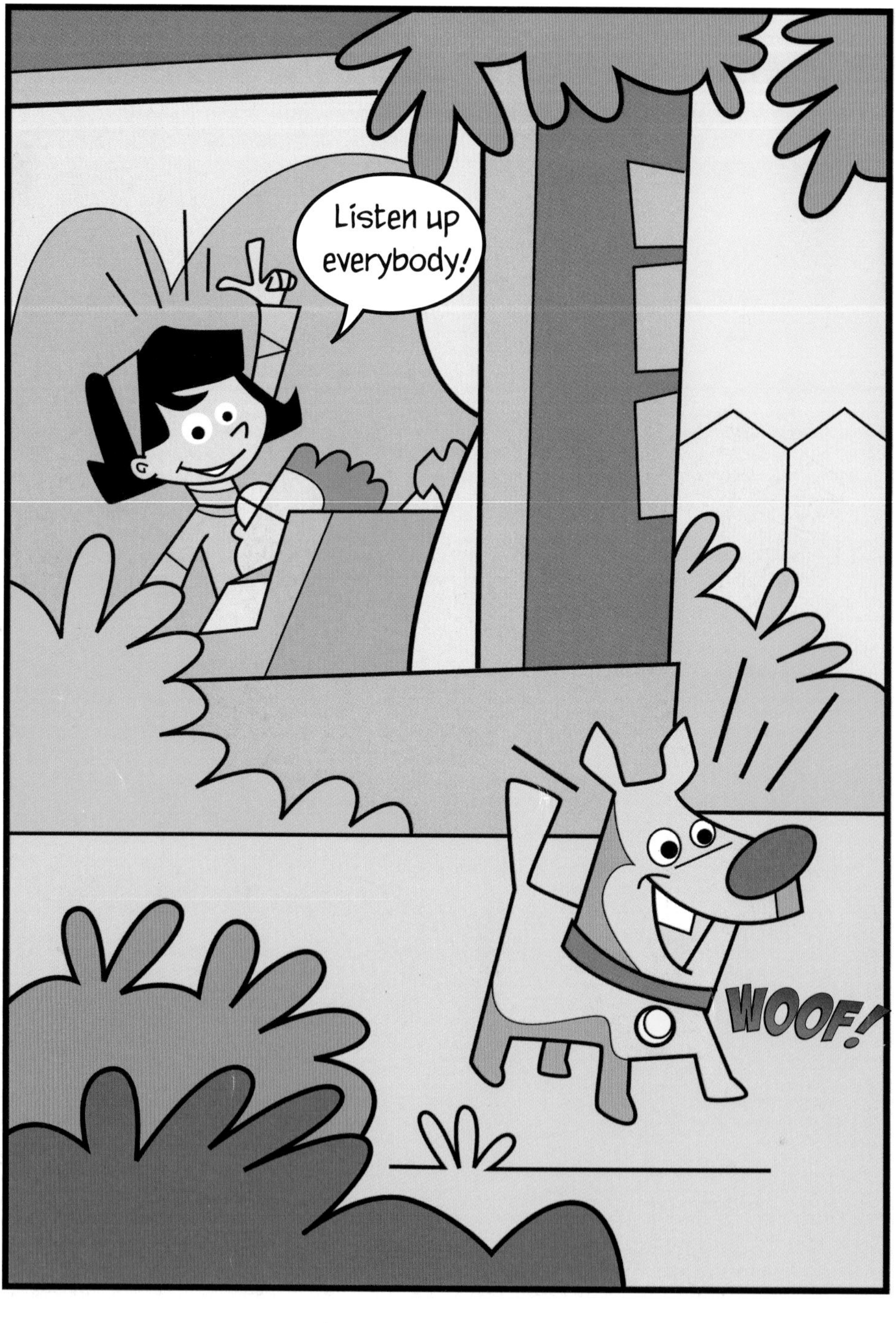
Listen up everybody!
WOOF!

Instead of having a pet show, they would become detectives.

Ava and her friends went back outside. They looked for clues.

They searched under all the chairs, but
Oatmeal wasn't there.

Suddenly, Ava heard a familiar noise.

They ran across the yard, but it wasn't Oatmeal.

It was the neighbor's cat.

The neighbor's cat ran away.

But Clair's dog kept barking. Ava wished he would stop.

Who could think about clues with all that noise?

Then Ava stopped covering her ears. She'd been ignoring the biggest and loudest clue of all!

Ava raced to the shed and opened the door.

Ava's pet show was a hit. Caleb's snake won a prize for the longest pet.

Clair's dog won for the loudest pet.

And Oatmeal won a prize for his disappearing act.

Lori Mortensen is a multi-published children's author who writes fiction and nonfiction on all sorts of subjects. When she's not plunking away at the keyboard, she enjoys making cheesy bread rolls, gardening, and hanging out with her family at their home in northern California.

Artist Rémy Simard began his career as an illustrator in 1980. Today he creates computer-generated illustrations for a large variety of clients. He has also written and illustrated more than 30 children's books in both French and English, including *Monsieur Noir et Blanc*, a finalist for Canada's Governor's Prize. To relax, Rémy likes to race around on his motorcycle. Rémy resides in Montreal with his two sons and a cat named Billy.

GLOSSARY

CLUES (KLOOZ) — things that help you find the answer to a mystery

DETECTIVES (di-TEK-tivz) — people who try to solve mysteries or crimes

DISAPPEARED (diss-up-PIHRD) — to go missing

FAMILIAR (fuh-MIL-yur) — something a person knows very well

IGNORING (ig-NOR-ing) — not paying attention to something

MYSTERY (MISS-tur-ee) — something that is hard to understand or explain

SEARCHED (SURCHD) — looked for something

DISCUSSION QUESTIONS

1. Do you have any pets? If so, what are they? If not, do you want a pet?

2. Ava decides she wants to have a pet show. Have you ever been part of a show? If so, what was it?

3. Do you want to be a detective? Why or why not?

WRITING PROMPTS

1. To find Oatmeal, Ava and her friends become detectives. Make a list of supplies you would need if you were a detective.

2. At the end of the story, each animal wins a prize. Make a new prize for each animal. Write down the new prizes and the reasons why each animal got the prize listed.

3. Did you know where Oatmeal was? Look through the book and write down clues you find.

MY 1ST GRAPHIC NOVEL®

THE 1ST STEP INTO GRAPHIC NOVELS

MY 1ST GRAPHIC NOVEL®

CLUES IN THE ATTIC

by Carl Meister
Illustrated by Rémy Simard

MYSTERY

These books are the perfect introduction to the world of safe, appealing graphic novels. Each story uses familiar topics, repeating patterns, and core vocabulary words appropriate for a beginning reader. Combine the entertaining story with comic book panels, exciting action elements, and bright colors and a safe graphic novel is born.

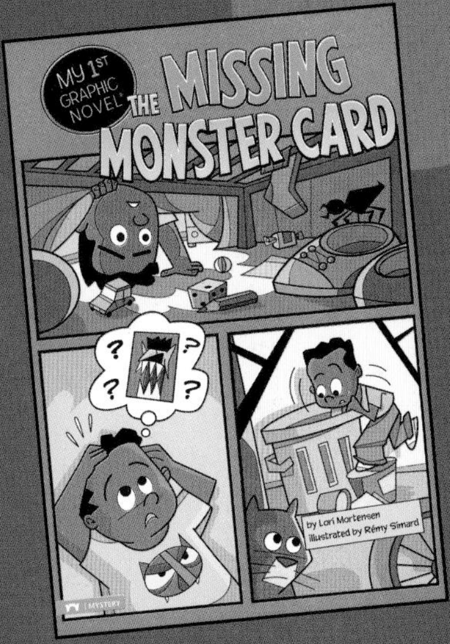
MY 1ST GRAPHIC NOVEL
THE MISSING MONSTER CARD
by Lori Mortensen
illustrated by Rémy Simard
MYSTERY

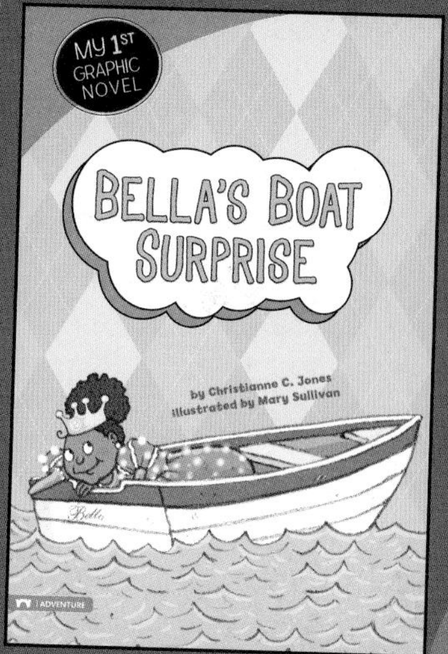
MY 1ST GRAPHIC NOVEL
BELLA'S BOAT SURPRISE
by Christianne C. Jones
illustrated by Mary Sullivan
ADVENTURE

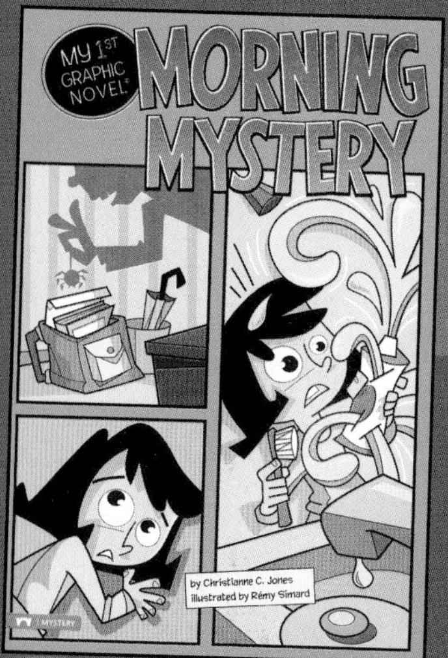
MY 1ST GRAPHIC NOVEL
MORNING MYSTERY
by Christianne C. Jones
illustrated by Rémy Simard
MYSTERY

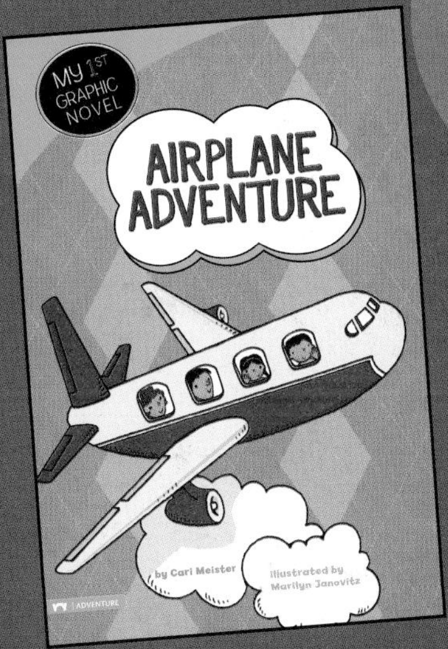
MY 1ST GRAPHIC NOVEL
AIRPLANE ADVENTURE
by Cari Meister
illustrated by Marilyn Janovitz
ADVENTURE

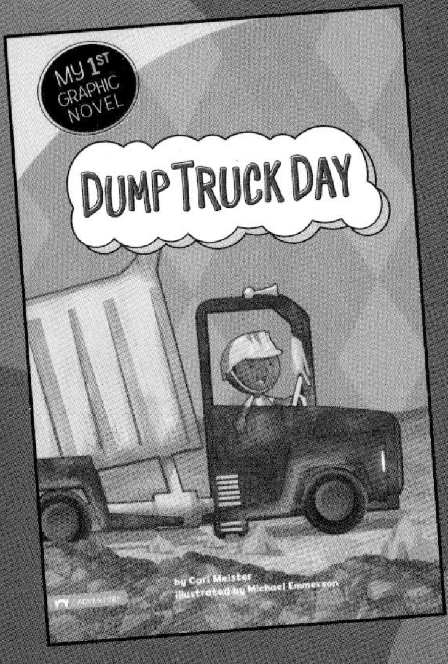
MY 1ST GRAPHIC NOVEL
DUMP TRUCK DAY
by Cari Meister
illustrated by Michael Emmerson
ADVENTURE

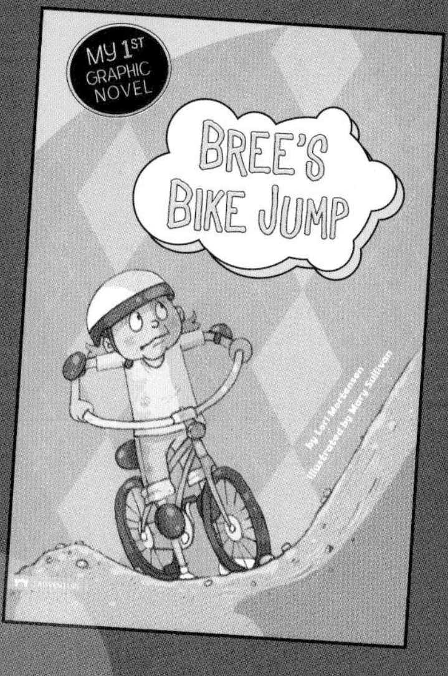
MY 1ST GRAPHIC NOVEL
BREE'S BIKE JUMP
by Lori Mortensen
illustrated by Mary Sullivan